Given by Matt Spahr
to Mr. Micciche
2008

Best wishes!

Happy reading!

Robert D. San Souci

· 2008 ·

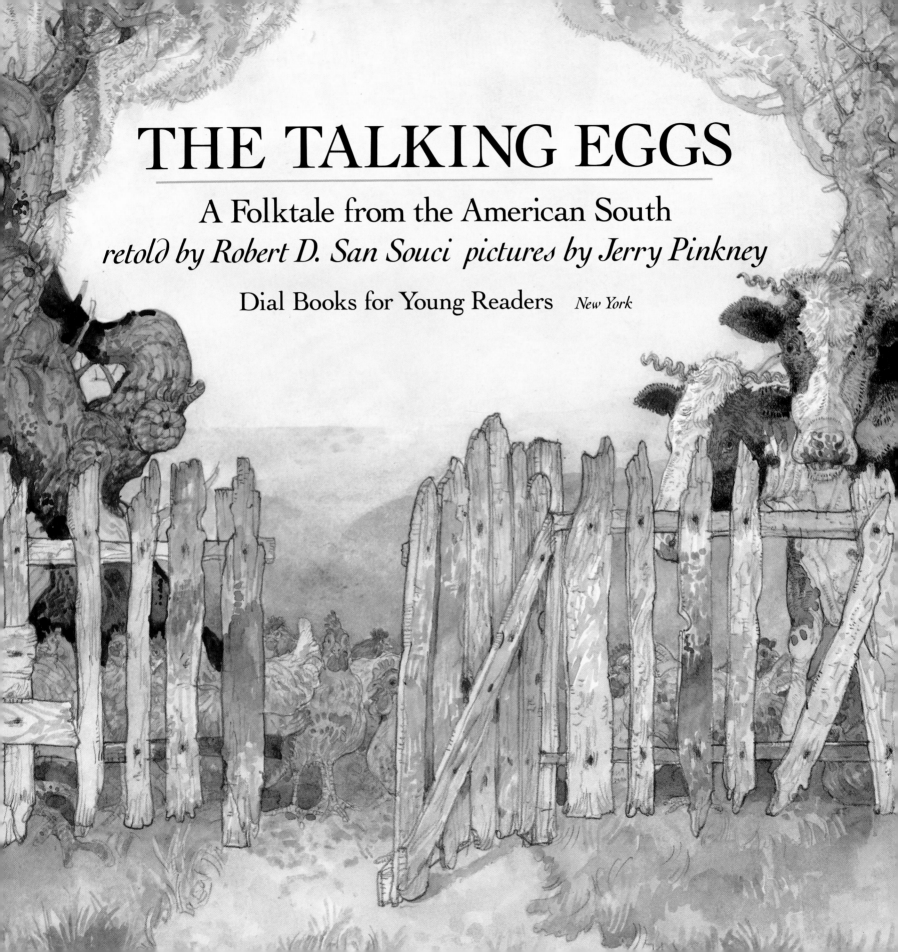

THE TALKING EGGS

A Folktale from the American South

retold by Robert D. San Souci   pictures by Jerry Pinkney

Dial Books for Young Readers   *New York*

Published by Dial Books for Young Readers
A division of Penguin Young Readers Group
345 Hudson Street
New York, New York 10014

Designed by Jane Byers Bierhorst
Manufactured in China by
South China Printing Company Limited
W
32 33 34 35 36 37 38 39 40

Library of Congress Cataloging in Publication Data
San Souci, Robert D. | The talking eggs
Summary | A Southern folktale in which
kind Blanche, following the instructions of
an old witch, gains riches, while her greedy
sister makes fun of the old woman
and is duly rewarded.
[1. Folklore — United States.]
I. Pinkney, Jerry, ill. II. Title.
PZ8.1.S227Tal   1989   398.2′1′0973   88-33469
ISBN 0-8037-0619-7 | ISBN 0-8037-0620-0 (lib. bdg.)

*The full-color artwork was prepared using pencil, colored pencils,
and watercolor. It was then color-separated and reproduced
as red, blue, yellow, and black halftones.*

*To Carol Toms, whose friendship and support
are constant in an inconstant world*
R.S.S.

To my granddaughter Charnelle
J.P.

The Talking Eggs is adapted from a Creole folktale originally
included in a collection of Louisiana stories by the folklorist
Alcee Fortier and published late in the nineteenth century. The tale
appears to have its roots in popular European fairy tales, probably
brought to Louisiana by French émigrés. Variations of the story,
with Cajun or Gullah overtones, suggest that it was gradually
spread orally through other areas of the American South.
R.S.S.

Back in the old days there was a widow with two daughters named Rose and Blanche. They lived on a farm so poor, it looked like the tail end of bad luck. They raised a few chickens, some beans, and a little cotton to get by.

Rose, the older sister, was cross and mean and didn't know beans from birds' eggs. Blanche was sweet and kind and sharp as forty crickets. But their mother liked Rose the best, because they were alike as two peas in a pod — bad-tempered, sharp-tongued, and always putting on airs.

The mother made Blanche do all the work around the place. She had to iron the clothes each morning using an old iron filled with hot coals, chop cotton in the afternoon, and string the beans for supper. While she'd be doing these chores, her mama and sister would sit side by side in rocking chairs on the shady porch, fanning themselves and talking foolishness about getting rich and moving to the city, where they could go to fancy balls wearing trail-train dresses and lots of jewels.

One hot day the mother sent Blanche to the well to fetch a bucket of water. When the girl got there, she found an old woman wrapped in a raggedy black shawl, near fainting with the heat.

"Please, child, give me a sip of water," the old woman said. "I'm 'bout to die of thirst."

"Yes, aunty," said Blanche, rinsing out her bucket and dipping up some clean, cool well water. "Drink what you need."

"Thank you, child," said the old woman when she'd taken swallow after swallow of water. "You got a spirit of do-right in your soul. God is gonna bless you." Then she walked away down the path that led to the deep woods.

When Blanche got back to the cabin, her mother and sister hollered at her for taking so long.

"This water's so warm, it's near boilin'," shouted Rose, and she dumped the bucket out on the porch.

"Here your poor sister's near dyin' for a drop of cool water," her mother screamed, "and you can't even bring her that little thing."

Then the two of them scolded and hit Blanche until the frightened girl ran away into the woods. She began to cry, since she didn't have anywhere to go, and she was scared to go home.

Suddenly, around a bend in the path came the old woman in the raggedy black shawl. When she saw Blanche, she asked kindly, "What's made you cry so, you poor child?"

"Mama and sister Rose lit into me for something that wasn't my fault," said Blanche, rubbing tears off her cheek. "Now I'm afraid to go home."

"Hush, child! Stop your crying. You come on home with me. I'll give you supper and a clean bed. But you got to promise you won't laugh at anything you see."

Blanche gave her word of honor that she wouldn't laugh. Then the old woman took her by the hand and led her deep into the backwoods. As they walked along the narrow path, bramble bushes and tree branches opened wide in front of them, and closed up behind them.

Soon they came to the old woman's tumbledown shack. A cow with two heads, and horns like corkscrews, peered over a fence at Blanche and brayed like a mule. She reckoned it was a pretty strange sight, but she didn't say anything, not wanting to hurt the old woman's feelings.

Next, she saw that the yard in front of the cabin was filled with chickens of every color. Some were hopping about on one leg, some running about on three or four or even more. These chickens didn't cluck, but whistled like mockingbirds. But strange as all this was, Blanche stuck by her promise not to laugh.

When they got inside the cabin, the old woman said, "Light the fire, child, and cook us some supper." So Blanche fetched kindling from the woodpile outside the back door.

The old woman sat down near the fireplace and took off her head. She set it on her knees like a pumpkin. First she combed out her gray hair, then she plaited it into two long braids. Blanche got pretty scared at this. But the woman had been nothing but kind to her, so she just went on lighting the fire.

After a bit the old woman put her head back on her shoulders and looked at herself in a sliver of mirror nailed to the cabin wall. "Um-m-m-hum!" she said, nodding. "That's better."

Then she gave Blanche an old beef bone and said, "Put this in the pot for supper."

Now Blanche was near starving, and the bone looked like a pretty sad meal for the two of them, but she did what the old woman said. "Shall I boil it for soup, aunty?" she asked.

"Look at the pot, child!" the old woman said, laughing.

The pot was filled with thick stew, bubbling away.

Next the woman gave Blanche only one grain of rice and told her to grind it in the stone mortar. Feeling mighty foolish Blanche began to pound the grain with the heavy stone pestle. In a moment the mortar was overflowing with rice.

When they had finished supper, the old woman said, "It's a fine moonshiny night, child. Come with me."

They sat themselves down on the back porch steps. After a time dozens of rabbits came out of the underbrush and formed a circle in the yard. The men rabbits all had frock-tail coats, and the lady rabbits had little trail-train dresses. They danced, standing on their hind feet, hopping about. One big rabbit played a banjo, and the old woman hummed along with it.

Blanche kept time by clapping along. The rabbits did a square dance, a Virginia reel, and even a cakewalk. The girl felt so happy, she never wanted to leave. She sat and clapped until she fell asleep, and the old woman carried her inside and put her to bed.

When Blanche got up the next morning, the old woman told her, "Go milk my cow."

The girl did what she was told and the two-headed cow with the curly horns gave her a bucket of the sweetest milk she'd ever tasted. They had it with their morning coffee.

"You gotta go home now, child," the old woman said to Blanche, who was washing the breakfast dishes. "But I tell you, things will be better from here on out. And since you are such a good girl, I got a present for you.

"Go out to the chicken house. Any eggs that say, 'Take me,' you go ahead and take. But if you hear any say, 'Don't take me,' you leave them be. When you get near home, throw those eggs one after another over your left shoulder so they break in the road behind you. Then you'll get a surprise."

When Blanche got to the little chicken house, she found all the nests filled with eggs. Half were gold or silver or covered with jewels; half looked no different from the eggs she got from her chickens back home.

All the plain eggs told her, "Take me." All the fancy ones cried, "Don't take me." She wished she could take just *one* gold or silver or jeweled egg, but she did what the old woman told her and only scooped up the plain ones.

She and the old woman waved good-bye to each other, then Blanche went on her way. Partway home she began to toss the eggs one at a time over her left shoulder. All sorts of wonderful things spilled out of those eggs: now diamonds and rubies, now gold and silver coins, now pretty silk dresses and dainty satin shoes. There was even a handsome carriage that grew in a wink from the size of a matchbox—and a fine brown-and-white pony that sprouted from the size of a cricket to draw it.

Blanche loaded all these lovely things into the carriage and rode the rest of the way home like a grand lady.

When she got back to the cabin, her mother and sister just gawked at her new finery. "Where did you get all these things?" her mother asked, making Rose help Blanche carry the treasures inside. That evening the mother cooked dinner for the first time since Blanche was old enough to hold a skillet. All the time telling Blanche what a sweet daughter she was, her mama got the girl to tell about the old woman and the cabin in the woods and the talking eggs.

When Blanche was asleep, the mother grabbed Rose and told her, "You gotta go into the woods tomorrow mornin' and find that old aunty. Then you'll get some of those talkin' eggs for yourse'f so's you can have fine dresses and jewels like your sister. When you get back, I'll chase Blanche off and keep her things myse'f. Then we'll go to the city and be fine ladies like we was meant to be."

"Can't we just run her off tonight so's I don't have to go pokin' through the woods lookin' for some crazy ol' aunty?" Rose whined.

"There's not near enough for two," her mother said, getting angry. "You do as I say and don't be so contrary."

So the next morning Rose set out drag-foot into the woods. She dawdled mostly, but soon met the old woman in her raggedy black shawl.

"My sweet little sister Blanche tol' me you got a real pretty house an' all," said Rose. "I'd 'preciate to see it."

"You can come with me if you've a mind to," said the old woman, "but you got to promise not to laugh at whatever you see."

"I swear," said Rose.

So the old woman led her through the bramble bushes and tree branches into the deep woods.

But when they got near the cabin and Rose saw the two-headed cow that brayed like a mule and the funny-looking chickens that sang like mockingbirds, she yelled, "If there ever was a sight, that's one! That's the stupidest thing in the world!" Then she laughed and laughed until she nearly fell down.

"Um-m-m-hum," said the old woman, shaking her head.

Inside, Rose complained when she was asked to start the fire, and she wound up with more smoke than flame. When the old woman gave her an old bone to put in the pot for supper, Rose said crossly, "That's gonna make a mighty poor meal." She dropped it in the pot, but the old bone remained a bone, so they only had thin soup for supper. When the old woman gave her one grain of rice to grind in the mortar, Rose said, "That sad speck won't hardly feed a fly!" She wouldn't lift the pestle, so they had no rice at all.

"Um-m-m-hum!" the old woman muttered.

Rose went to bed hungry. All night long she heard mice scratching under the floor and screech-owls clawing at the window.

In the morning the old woman told her to milk the cow. Rose did, but she made fun of the two-headed creature and all she got was a little sour milk not fit for drinking. So they had their breakfast coffee without cream.

When the old woman lifted her head off her shoulders to brush her hair, quick as a wink Rose grabbed that head and said, "I'm not gonna put you back t'gether 'til you give me presents like my sister got."

"Ah, child, you're a wicked girl," said the old woman's head, "but I got to have my body back, so I'll tell you what to do.

"Go to the chicken house and take those eggs that say, 'Take me.' But leave be the ones that cry, 'Don't take me.' Then you toss those eggs over your right shoulder when you're on your way home."

To be sure the old woman wasn't playing her a trick, Rose set the old woman's head out on the porch while her body sat groping around the cabin. Then she ran to the chicken house. Inside, all the plain eggs cried, "Take me," while all the gold and silver and jeweled ones said, "Don't take me."

"You think I'm fool enough to listen to you and pass up the prettiest ones? Not on your life!" So she grabbed all of the gold and silver and jeweled eggs that kept yelling, "Don't take me," and off she ran into the woods with them.

As soon as she was out of sight of the old woman's cabin, she tossed the eggs over her right shoulder as fast as she could. But out of the shells came clouds of whip snakes, toads, frogs, yellow jackets, and a big, old, gray wolf. These began to chase after her like pigs after a pumpkin.

Hollering bloody murder Rose ran all the way to her mother's cabin. When the woman saw the swarm of things chasing her daughter, she tried to rescue her with a broom. But the wasps and wolf and all the other creatures wouldn't be chased off, so mother and daughter hightailed it to the woods, with all the animals following.

When they returned home, angry and sore and stung and covered with mud, they found Blanche had gone to the city to live like a grand lady—though she remained as kind and generous as always.

For the rest of their lives Rose and her mother tried to find the strange old woman's cabin and the talking eggs, but they never could find that place again.